DISCARD

The Catlady

ALSO AVAILABLE BY DICK KING-SMITH

FOR OLDER READERS

DICK KING-SMITH

ᶜᵗʰᵉ Catlady

Illustrated by John Eastwood

Alfred A. Knopf
NEW YORK

THIS IS A BORZOI BOOK PUBLISHED BY ALFRED A. KNOPF
Text copyright © 2004 by Fox Busters Ltd.
Illustrations copyright © 2004 by John Eastwood
Jacket illustration copyright © 2006 by Wayne Parmenter

All rights reserved under International and Pan-American Copyright Conventions.
Published in the United States by Alfred A. Knopf, an imprint of Random House
Children's Books, a division of Random House, Inc., New York. Distributed by
Random House, Inc., New York. Originally published in Great Britain by Doubleday,
an imprint of Random House Children's Books, in 2004.

www.randomhouse.com/kids

KNOPF, BORZOI BOOKS, and the colophon are registered trademarks of Random
House, Inc.

Library of Congress Cataloging-in-Publication Data
King-Smith, Dick.
The catlady / Dick King-Smith ; illustrated by John Eastwood.
p. cm.
SUMMARY: Muriel Ponsonby, the Catlady, lives with dozens of cats, many of whom
she believes are reincarnated friends, relatives, and even royalty.
ISBN 0-375-82985-7 (trade) — ISBN 0-375-92985-1 (lib. bdg.)
[1. Cats—Fiction. 2. Reincarnation—Fiction. 3. England—Fiction.] I. Eastwood, John,
ill. II. Title.
PZ7.K5893 Cat 2006
[Fic]—dc22
2005009507

Printed in the United States of America
January 2006
10 9 8 7 6 5 4 3 2 1
First American Edition

Chapter One

On the morning of January 22, 1901, Muriel Ponsonby had, living in her house, sixteen cats (including kittens). By the evening of that day, another litter of kittens had been born, bringing the total to a round twenty.

This event was, as usual, recorded in a large book titled BIRTHDAY BOOK (CATS ONLY).

Miss Ponsonby, it should be explained, was an elderly lady living alone in a large country house that had belonged to her parents. Because she had always looked after them, she had never married, and after their deaths she had allowed her liking for cats

1

full rein. To be sure, she gave away some of the many kittens that appeared, but nevertheless Ponsonby Place—for this was the name of the family home—was always swarming with cats.

Miss Ponsonby kept herself to herself and did not mix much with the local villagers, save to go now and then to the shop to buy provisions for herself and the cats. Most felt she was harmless, a rather sweet old lady, but there were some who said she was a witch. Partly because of this, she was known to one and all as "the Catlady."

In fact, she was not a witch but simply a somewhat strange old woman with odd habits.

For example, she talked constantly throughout the day—to herself, a listener might have thought. But this was no sign of madness. She was, of course, talking to her cats, and they talked back. Colonel Sir Percival Ponsonby and his wife had always addressed their daughter by a shortened version of her Christian name, Muriel, and all her cats used this. When spoken to, they would reply, "Mu! Mu! Mu!"

Many would have found it odd to discover that she took all her meals with her cats. The long refectory table in the great dining room was laid with a bowl for each adult cat and any kittens old enough to jump up on it, and the Catlady would sit at the head with her own bowl before her.

To be sure, she used a knife and fork and spoon, and afterward wiped her lips with a napkin while the rest cleaned their faces with their paws. But on occasion, so as not to seem standoffish, she would fill a bowl with milk and lap from it.

At nighttime she was kept very comfortable, especially in the winter, for all those cats who wished—and many did—slept on her bed, providing her with a warm, furry bedspread.

With her rather sharp features, green eyes, and gray hair tied back to show her

somewhat pointed ears, Muriel Ponsonby looked much like a giant cat as she lay stretched beneath the purring throng.

Few people knew of her eating habits, for she had no servants, and only the doctor, called on a rare occasion when she was confined to bed, had ever seen the cat blanket. But no one at all knew the strangest thing about Miss Ponsonby, which was that she was a firm believer in reincarnation.

As a simple soldier, her father, who had served in the army in India, thought that the idea of reincarnation was a lot of nonsense, but he had talked about it to his daughter when she was a child. As she grew older, Muriel came to believe, as Hindus do, that when a person dies, he or she is reborn in another body, and not necessarily a human one. She was sure that some of her feline companions had once been people she knew. Thus among her cats there was a Percival (her late father, she was certain, just the same whiskers), a Florence (her late mother), a Rupert and a Madeleine (cousins), a Walter and a Beatrice (uncle and aunt), as well as some newly departed friends. Ethel Simmons, Margaret Maitland, and Edith Wilson (two tabbies and a black), all old school friends of hers, had reappeared in feline form.

It was to these nine cats that Muriel Ponsonby chiefly spoke, and they replied by making typical cat noises like meowing and purring. All were delighted to be living in comfort in Ponsonby Place, in the care of a human whom they had, in their previous lives, known and loved.

Percival and Florence were, of course, particularly pleased at how well their only daughter had turned out.

"How fortunate we are, my dear," the Colonel said to his wife, "to be looked after by Muriel in our old age."

"Old age?" said Florence. "I think you tend to forget, Percival, that we have been reincarnated into new bodies and that ours are now comparatively young."

"You are right, of course, Florence dear," Percival replied. "Why, we have our new lives ahead of us."

"And possibly other lives," said Florence.

"What do you mean?"

Florence rubbed her face against her husband's luxuriant whiskers. "We might have babies," she said.

Of course, not all the kittens born in Ponsonby Place were reincarnations of human beings. Most were simply ordinary kittens born to ordinary cats and were given names like Tibbles or Fluff. The Catlady could tell the difference merely by looking into their eyes once they were opened, and until this happened she did not attempt to name them.

So it was not for ten days that she examined the four kittens born on January 22, 1901, the very day upon which Queen Victoria had died. Three of the kittens were tabbies, the fourth a ginger.

The Catlady picked up the tabbies first, looking to see what sex each was and then peering into its newly opened eyes.

"You're a tom," she said three times, and, again three times, "Sorry, dear, you're only a cat."

But when she came to the fourth kitten, a small and dumpy one, expecting it to be another tom—for ginger kittens usually were—she found it to be a queen, as female cats are called. Then she looked into its eyes and caught her breath.

"Not just a queen," said the Catlady in a hoarse whisper, "but *the* Queen!"

Reverently, she placed the ginger kitten back in its nest. "Oh, Your Majesty!" she said. "Reborn on the day you died! To think that you have come to grace my house!" And awkwardly, for she was not as young as she had been, she dropped a curtsy.

"Your humble servant, ma'am," said the Catlady, and retired from the room, backward.

Chapter Two

Hastily, the Catlady made her way from the room in the East Wing where this latest litter of kittens had been born to the principal bedroom of Ponsonby Place. It was a spacious chamber where her parents had slept in their lifetime—their previous lifetime, that is—and that they, in their reborn shapes, still naturally occupied. Once the Colonel had been a fiery old soldier and his wife a bit of a battle-ax, and now no other cat ever dared cross this threshold.

The Catlady found them lying side by side in the middle of the great four-poster bed. Percival had been reincarnated as a white kitten that had grown into a very large and fat cat. His sweeping whiskers aped the military mustache of the human Percival. Florence was a tortoiseshell with just the same small, dark eyes that had once glinted behind Lady Ponsonby's pince-nez.

"Papa! Mama!" cried the Catlady excitedly (she could never bring herself to address them by their first names). At the sound of her voice, they yawned and stretched themselves upon the fine silken bedspread with its pattern of damask roses, which was now much torn by sharp claws and dirtied by muddy feet.

"What do you think!" went on the Catlady. "Our dear departed Queen is come to stay! Edward VII may now be King of England, but here at Ponsonby Place Victoria still reigns!"

"Mu," said Percival in a bored voice, and Florence echoed, "Mu." And they climbed off the four-poster and made their way down the curving staircase toward the dining room, for it was time for tea.

How I wish Mama and Papa were still able to speak the Queen's English—the King's English, I should say, mused the Catlady as, in the huge stone-flagged kitchen, she set about the task of filling a large number of bowls with a mixture of fish heads and boiled rabbit and ox liver. For that matter, I wish that those others that have been reborn could speak too. How nice it would be to talk over old times with Uncle Walter and Aunt Beatrice or chat about school days with Ethel or one of the other girls.

Her thoughts were interrupted by a loud, impatient meowing from the waiting cats.

The Catlady sighed. "Coming, dears!" she called.

She sat at the head of the table, nibbling a biscuit. Later, when all had been cleared away and washed up, she would make herself a nice cup of tea, but at that moment she realized for the first time that she was not only lonely for human conversation but that she was tired.

The older I get, she thought, the more cats and so the more work I have, and it'll be worse soon. Both Cousin Madeleine and Edith Wilson are pregnant.

By the time she got to bed that night (after paying her respects to the infant Queen Victoria), the Catlady had come to a decision. "There's only one thing for it, dears," she said to the patchwork quilt of different-colored cats that covered her. "I shall have to get help."

The next day she composed an advertisement to be placed in the local newspaper, the *Dummerset Chronicle*. It was very short. It said:

For some days the Catlady waited, rather nervously, for replies. She had been a recluse for so many years now that she was not looking forward to the ordeal of interviewing a whole string of strange people.

She need not have worried. As soon as the locals of Dumpton Muddicorum read the "Situations Vacant" in the *Dummerset Chronicle,* they said to each other, "Look at this, then! It's the old Catlady, advertising for home help. What a job, eh? Great rambling place, crawling with cats, and stinking of them too, no doubt. And as for her, well, if she ain't a witch she's as mad as a hatter! Anyone who applies for that needs their heads seen to."

And no one did.

Muriel Ponsonby did not renew the advertisement. Perhaps it's just as well, she thought. I probably wouldn't have got on with the person. I'll just have to manage somehow.

Nonetheless, when shopping in the village, she did ask the shopkeepers if they knew of anyone suitable, but none of them did.

"Not at the moment, madam," said the butcher, tipping his straw hat to her, "but I'll be sure to let you know if I hear of anyone." And the others replied in the same vein. They winked at other customers when she had left their shops, and the customers smiled and shook their heads, watching her pedal rather shakily away on her tall black bicycle with the big wicker basket on the handlebars.

Poor old dear, they thought. She needs some help, no doubt about that, but she'll be lucky to get anyone. Shame, really, she's a nice old thing.

As for the village children, they sniggered behind their hands. "It's that old Catlady!" they whispered. And when she had gone by, they curled their fingers like claws and hissed and catcalled, pretending to scratch one another.

The weeks went by, and Cousin Madeleine and Edith Wilson both gave birth, one to four and one to six kittens. These were just ordinary kittens (for no one among the Catlady's family or friends had died), but with a total now of thirty animals in her house, she found herself wishing very much that someone—anyone—had answered that advertisement.

By now the little tubby ginger female that was, its owner knew beyond doubt, the reincarnation of the late great Queen was weaned. The Catlady found that, try as she would to treat all her animals alike, this one had already become special. She took to carrying her about and had at long last decided what to call her.

After the first shock of finding who was within the little furry body, she had very gradually given up treating this kitten with such exaggerated respect. She stopped curtsying to it and backing out of the room. From first addressing it as "Your Majesty," she had then progressed to "Victoria" and later, so familiar did she now feel with this royal personage, to "Vicky."

The other cats, incidentally, on learning from the ginger kitten who she had been in her previous incarnation, treated her with much respect—Percival especially so, as in his former shape, his bravery in India had earned him the Victoria Cross.

One winter's day, when the snow lay deep around Ponsonby Place, there was a knocking on the great front door, and the Catlady went to see who it could be, Vicky perched upon her shoulder.

Muriel opened the door, expecting the postman, for no one else usually came all the way up the long drive to the house. But it wasn't the postman. Standing on the steps outside was a young girl, poorly clad and shivering with cold.

Though on the whole the Catlady preferred cats to people, she was of a kindly nature, and now she did not hesitate. "Come in! Come in!" she cried. "You'll catch your death, whoever you are. Come, follow me, I have a good fire in the drawing room." As the girl followed her across the vast, echoing hall, a host of cats watched curiously from doorway and stairway.

"Here, sit by the fire and warm yourself," said the Catlady, "and I will go and make you a hot drink."

When she had done so and the girl had drunk and some color had come back into her pinched face, the Catlady said, "Now tell me, what can I do for you?"

As she said this, it occurred to her that perhaps the girl had come in answer to that old advertisement in the *Dummerset Chronicle*. I rather hope not, the Catlady said to herself. This is not the sort of person I had in mind. Not only is she badly dressed but her clothes are dirty, with bits of straw sticking to them.

The Catlady's face must have shown her distaste, for the girl stood up and said, "I won't trouble you any longer, madam. I'll be on my way now, and thank you for your kindness."

She spoke with a Dummerset accent. A local girl, thought the Catlady. "Wait a moment," she said. "You knocked on my door, so you must tell me what you wanted."

"I saw your lights," said the girl, "and what with the snow . . . and I was fair wore out . . . and I hadn't eaten for quite a while . . . I just couldn't go any further."

"And you're not going any further now," said the Catlady decidedly. "Sit down again. I'll fetch you some food."

Chapter Three

Muriel Ponsonby was not particularly interested in food. As long as her cats were well fed, she herself was content with very simple fare, and she seldom kept much in the house.

Now, however, she was not long in providing some good hot soup and some bread and cheese for the young stranger, and not until the girl had finished eating did she press her further.

"Now tell me your name."

"If you please, madam," said the girl, "my name is Mary Nutt."

"But tell me, Mary," said the Catlady,

"where are your parents?" Mary's not very old, she thought. Fourteen, perhaps?

"Dead," Mary replied.

"Both?"

"Yes, madam. Mother died a month ago, and my father, he was killed in South Africa, fighting the Boers. He was a soldier, my dad was, a soldier of the Queen."

At this last word, Vicky jumped up onto the girl's lap, and Mary stroked her and added, "And the Queen's dead too now."

Yes and no, said the Catlady to herself.

To Mary she said, "I am very sorry for you. My father is . . . that is to say, was . . . a soldier."

And now he's a white cat, she thought.

"Thank you, madam," said Mary Nutt. "The fact is that since Mother died, I've had nowhere to live. These last weeks I've just just been wandering about the countryside, sleeping in haystacks, as you can see, with no food to speak of, for I've no money. That was the first good meal I've had for many a day, and I thank you for your kindness."

This telling of her troubles and the sight of Vicky snuggled down on the girl's lap would probably have been enough to make up the Catlady's mind anyway. But then something happened that absolutely decided her.

In through the drawing room door marched the white cat Percival, straight up to the girl, and he began to rub himself against her legs, purring like mad.

Mary Nutt put out a hand to stroke him. "Isn't he handsome!" she said.

"You like cats, do you?" asked the Colonel's daughter.

"Oh yes!" replied the daughter of a trooper.

The Catlady looked at her, stroking with one hand Colonel Sir Percival Ponsonby and with the other cuddling Victoria, Queen of the United Kingdom, Empress of India, and any doubts vanished. "I hope," she said, "that you will stay here with me, Mary, and help me to look after my family."

On that snowy day when Mary Nutt first set foot in Ponsonby Place, the house was as it had been for many years now. That is to say, the floors were dirty, the ceilings cobwebby, the furniture dusty, the chair covers grubby, and the windows smeary.

The place was a paradise for cockroaches and wood lice and earwigs and beetles and even, in the damper parts, for snails (though mice had the sense to keep well away).

On top of everything else, the whole house stank of cat.

By springtime the change in Ponsonby Place was miraculous. The floors and the ceilings and the furniture were clean, the covers washed, the insects gone. If the Colonel and his lady could have been reincarnated in human rather than feline form, the house would have looked to them just as it had been in their day. To be sure, there was still a smell of cat, but, thanks to opening as many (clean) windows as possible when the weather allowed, it was much less strong now.

All this, of course, was due to the busy hands of Mary Nutt, who had turned out to be what the Catlady's mother would have called "a treasure."

At first from simple gratitude at being given a home and then because she quickly grew fond of the Catlady, Mary worked from dawn to dusk in Ponsonby Place, dusting, scrubbing, washing, and polishing, and indeed doing most of the cooking. Even more importantly from the Catlady's point of view, her new helper paid a

lot of attention to all the cats, and whenever she had a spare moment, it was spent grooming some happily purring puss.

Percival and the rest spoke about her to each other with approval. "Good sort of girl, that, don't you think?" he said to Florence. "She's being a great help to Mu, what?" And his wife agreed, as did the uncle and aunt, the cousins, and the school friends. Only Vicky made no comment.

The Colonel cleared his throat.

"I hope you approve of the young servant, Your Majesty?" he said respectfully.

Vicky looked up at the big white cat with her usual haughty expression. "We have only one criticism," she replied.

"What is that, pray, ma'am?"

"We do not have enough attention paid to us. We are, after all, the most important cat in the house—in the land, indeed. The girl should feed us first."

"Certainly she should, ma'am," said Percival, and once Vicky had left the room, he had a word with all the other cats.

From then on, to Mary's puzzlement and Muriel's delight, when the food bowls were put upon the long refectory table, no cat touched a mouthful of its food until the tubby ginger cat Vicky had finished her meal and jumped down.

Just as it should be, thought the Catlady. Her Majesty must eat first. Perhaps one of these days I'll tell Mary about reincarnation. The poor girl has lost both father and mother, or at least she thinks she has. It would surely be a comfort if I could persuade her that each of them is no doubt enjoying another life in another form.

Chapter Four

As time passed, the relationship between the Catlady and her young orphaned helper strengthened.

Miss Muriel (as Mary now addressed her employer) became a kind of replacement for the girl's late mother, despite the huge gap in age.

Equally, for the childless Catlady, this hard-working, affectionate, cat-loving girl was a great blessing. Especially because once again the cat population of Ponsonby Place was increasing. Margaret Maitland and Edith Wilson had, between them, another half dozen kittens, so that now the total was thirty-six.

Miss Muriel was pleased with the new arrivals, Mary could see, though she did not understand why the Catlady had picked up each new kitten, peered into its eyes, and then said in a disappointed voice, "Oh dear, you're just a cat."

Just another cat, Mary thought, and more work for me. She knew, because she'd been told, that when the Colonel and Lady Ponsonby had been alive, they had employed a cook, a parlormaid, and three housemaids, and of course there had not been an army of cats in the place. If only I could persuade Miss Muriel, Mary thought, to get rid of some of them. Every bit of furniture is covered in cat hair, in wet weather every floor is dotted with muddy little pawprints, there are litter trays everywhere to be emptied, and often the kittens don't use them. What can I do to get Miss Muriel to part with some of them?

As though in answer to this question, a cat walked into the room Mary was dusting. It was a tomcat, she could see from its big, round face, and ebony in color. A black male, thought Mary Nutt. "Blackmail!" she said out loud.

Suppose I told Miss Muriel, she thought, that if a lot of the cats don't go, then I will? I wouldn't actually go, of course—I couldn't let her down like that when she's been so good to me—but it might just work. And we could shut up some of the rooms so there'd be less cleaning to do. Let's just hope I can persuade her.

As things turned out, luck was to be on Mary's side. While she was plucking up the courage to tackle her employer, the Catlady was herself beginning to feel that perhaps there were rather too many cats in Ponsonby Place. It's not the expense of feeding them, she said to herself—I don't mind that—and it's not the work involved, for now dear Mary prepares their food and washes their dishes and cleans out their litter trays. It's because of Vicky, I suppose. She's become so important to me (well, she would be, wouldn't she, she is ... was ... the Queen) that I don't pay as much attention to the others as I used to. Except for Papa and Mama, of course, and the relations and friends. But as for the rest of them, I suppose I could do without them. That cat blanket's getting too much of a thing. I'd sooner just have Her Majesty on the bed.

But then something happened that was to settle things for both Mary and Muriel. For some time the Catlady had been a trifle worried about her late mother (that is to say, about the tortoiseshell cat Florence, within whose body Lady Ponsonby had been reincarnated) because she seemed to be getting a bit fat.

"Oh, Mama," said the Catlady as she entered the master bedroom, carrying Vicky, "I shall have to feed you less. Just look at the tummy on you!"

Following her own advice, she looked

more carefully and then gave a gasp of horror as the truth dawned upon her.

"Oh, Mama!" she cried. "You are pregnant!"

Florence stretched languidly on the four-poster bed, and Percival purred proudly.

"And at your time of life!" said the Catlady.

Then she realized that though her mother if still alive would have been in her nineties, the cat she had become was young. What's more, when the coming kittens were born to Percival and Florence (to Papa and Mama, that is to say), they would be, strictly speaking, her own little brothers and sisters!

She hurried downstairs to the kitchen. "Mary! Mary!" she cried. "She is going to have kittens!"

"Who, Miss Muriel?"

In the nick of time, the Catlady stopped herself from replying, "My mama."

"My Florence!" she said. "I had thought she was just putting on too much weight, but now I see what it is!"

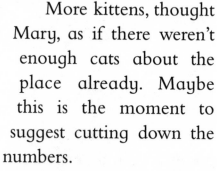

More kittens, thought Mary, as if there weren't enough cats about the place already. Maybe this is the moment to suggest cutting down the numbers.

"Wouldn't it be a good idea to get rid of a few of your cats, Miss Muriel?" she asked.

"Get rid of them?"

"Yes. Find good homes for them."

"But how?"

"I could put an advertisement in the local paper."

A few days later readers of the *Dummerset Chronicle* saw the following notice:

NUMBER OF CATS AND KITTENS,
FREE TO GOOD HOMES.
Apply Mary Nutt,
Ponsonby Place,
Dumpton Muddicorum,
Dummerset.

"You don't have to do anything, Miss Muriel," Mary said. "I give you my word I'll make sure they go to good homes."

In the next few weeks a lot of people came walking, cycling, or riding up the drive to Ponsonby Place. Some owned a cat but fancied having another, some had lost their cats and wanted to replace them, some had never owned a cat before but were attracted by that one word FREE. Many were just

35

curious and keen to take this chance to see the Catlady in her own home.

Such was the demand that soon Mary was having to turn people away. She pinned a notice on the front door that said:

"All those that have gone have got good homes, I'm sure, Miss Muriel," she said to the Catlady, who was sitting in an armchair in the drawing room with the Queen of the United Kingdom on her lap, reading a book called *The Care of Cats.*

"Well done, Mary dear," the Catlady said. "Though I shall miss them all very much."

Let's hope, she thought, that my Florence (Mama, that is) has a lot of kittens.

As though to compensate for the losses, Florence gave birth the very next day, on the fine silken bedspread of the four-poster in the bedroom of the Catlady's late parents.

"Oh, Mama!" breathed Muriel Ponsonby as she bent over the two newborn kittens. One was a tortoiseshell like the mother, the other white like the father, who sat nearby, purring with pride.

The Catlady had been an only child, but now she thought, I have a baby brother and a baby sister!

"Oh, Papa," she said, "what shall we call them?" But of course Percival merely replied, "Mu."

"I'll ask Mary," said the Catlady, and she followed Vicky (who always liked to lead the way) down to the kitchen.

If only Mary knew, she thought as she

told the good tidings, that these two new kittens are the children of my dear mama and papa, so that now I have the brother and the sister I never had as a child.

"Come up and see them," she said. And then as they stood looking down, she said, "What shall we call them? Why don't you choose, Mary Nutt?"

Mary laughed.

"We could call them after some sort of nut!" she said.

"What a good idea," said the Catlady. "Let's see now, there's walnut and peanut . . ."

". . . and chestnut and beechnut and groundnut . . ."

". . . and coconut and hazelnut," said the Catlady.

"Hazel," said Mary. "That would be a nice name for the little female, wouldn't it?"

"Oh yes!" said the Catlady. "But what about the little tom?"

"Coco, Miss Muriel," said Mary. "Short for *coconut*."

"I like it!" cried the Catlady.

My sister Hazel, she thought, and my brother Coco. What fun! How lucky I am to believe in reincarnation. It would be nice for Mary to  believe too. Just think. Her father, for instance—Arthur, I think he was called—suppose he's now a boy or a horse, perhaps, or a dog or maybe even something as small as a mouse. No, not a mouse, they don't live long enough. He'd

have gone into yet another body by now, dead of old age or, worse, killed by a cat. Just think, if dear Papa had eaten Arthur Nutt!

But it might help Mary, she said to herself, to know that I, at least, believe that her father is not dead and gone. His body might be buried on some South African battlefield, but his personality, his spirit, his soul, call it what you like, has been reincarnated, has entered some other body. Maybe I should try to explain it to her.

"Mary dear, tell me, is it very painful for you to talk of your parents?"

"Painful?" replied Mary. "Yes, it will always be painful. But they've gone. I just have to accept that."

"Gone," said the Catlady. "Gone where?"

"To Heaven, I suppose. They were good people."

"Have you ever thought," asked the Catlady, "that they might have been reincarnated?"

"What does that mean?"

"That they might have been reborn, in some other shape or form?"

"Oh, I don't think I could believe in that," Mary said.

"I do," said the Catlady.

Mary Nutt looked at her employer, the elderly, green-eyed Catlady, gray hair tied back as usual. She's aged quite a bit in the time I've lived here, she thought— rather bent, a bit unsteady on her feet—but her mind is still clear, I think.

Or rather, I thought. But this reincarnation thing!

"Do you mean," Mary asked, "that you believe you were someone else in a previous life?"

"Someone. Or perhaps somebody. I wasn't necessarily human."

"You could have been an animal?"

"Yes, indeed. I may be one in the future, when my heart stops beating. I don't expect you to believe in the idea, Mary, but I thought it might be a comfort to you to know that I am sure your mother and father are still enjoying lives of some sort. As indeed my dear mama and papa are."

"Your mother and father?"

"At this moment they are in their old bedroom, resting upon their four-poster bed, while my brother and sister play on the floor."

"I don't understand," said Mary.

"Percival and Florence. My father and mother."

"Those were their names?"

"Those are their names. New forms they may have

41

acquired, but I know without a shadow of a doubt who they were before they became cats. Just as I am absolutely certain about Vicky here. She was born at twenty past four on the afternoon of January 22, 1901, the very instant that the last breath left her previous body."

"Whose body was that?" Mary asked.

"Vicky, as I most disrespectfully call her, is in fact Victoria, Queen of the United Kingdom and Empress of India," said the Catlady.

She picked up the stout ginger cat and began, with great deference, to stroke her. "So now you know, Mary," she said. "Vicky here is the late great Queen Victoria."

Did I tell myself her mind was clear? Mary thought. She's barmy.

Chapter Five

The shopkeepers in Dumpton Muddicorum had always thought Miss Ponsonby a bit mad. "You'd have to be," they said, "to keep as many cats (and spend as much money on their food) as the Catlady does."

Nonetheless, they were still rather fond of her. She was always smiling, always polite. "She may be a bit strange," they said among themselves, "but she's a proper lady."

Of course, they knew nothing of her belief in reincarnation, but commented, first, on her kindness in giving away some of her cats ("Free," they said. "She never asked for a penny") and, secondly, on the fact that the years seemed to be telling on her. Riding her bicycle was patently becoming a big effort.

"Good job she's got that nice young girl living with her, what's her name ... Mary ... Mary Nutt, that's it," they said. They had not been surprised when Mary appeared in the village one day, riding the Catlady's tall black bicycle, to do the shopping. They each made regular inquiries of Mary as to how Miss Ponsonby was getting on.

One day Mary came back from the village to find the Catlady standing at the

front door, leaning on the walking stick that she now always used, and looking, Mary could see, very worried.

"What is it, Miss Muriel?" Mary asked before beginning to unload the shopping from the big wicker basket on the handlebars. "What's the matter?"

"Oh, Mary!" cried the Catlady. "It's my brother!"

"Your brother?"

"Yes, Coco. I can't find him anywhere. I've asked Mama and Papa and my sister Hazel where Coco has gone, but of course they couldn't tell me. Could he have been stolen, d'you think, or run away? I've searched the house but I can't find him."

"He must be somewhere about," Mary said. "I'll just unload this shopping and then I'll make you a nice cup of tea. I'll find him, don't you worry."

In fact, the white kitten Coco, adventurous as most boys are, had decided to do
some exploring.

In the master bedroom of Ponsonby
Place, there was a large fireplace, once used
to keep Sir Percival and Lady Ponsonby
warm on winter nights. When Coco was
alone in the room, he began to nose around
it. Looking up, he saw the sky through the

chimney stack. He also saw that there were
little stone steps on the walls of the chimney,
steps up which, long ago, children had been
sent to sweep down the soot with bags full of
goose feathers. Coco began to climb. As he
did so, the soot began to fall and he became

covered in the stuff. It got in his eyes and his nose and his mouth, and he became very frightened. He did not know whether to go on up or to come back down or what to do. He sat on one of the steps, mewing pitifully for his mother.

He was there, of course, when the Catlady was searching for him, but her hearing was too poor to catch his muffled cries and her eyesight not sharp enough to notice the fallen soot in the fireplace.

But Mary, when she began to search, both heard the kitten and saw the sootfall. Cautiously she peered up the chimney and saw the crouching figure of the tiny adventurer.

"Oh, Coco!" she called. "However are you going to get out of there?" The answer was immediate.

Perhaps it was the sight of her face, perhaps the sound of her voice, perhaps he simply lost his footing, but the next minute Coco came tumbling down into the fireplace.

Mary, by now very sooty herself, carried him down to the kitchen, where the Catlady still sat over her cup of tea.

"Here he is!" she said.

"But, Mary," the Catlady cried, peering through her spectacles, "my brother Coco is a white kitten, like Papa, and that one is coal-black."

"*Coal*-black's about right," Mary said, and she set about cleaning the unhappy Coco while on the floor below the sink, his parents watched and waited.

"Whatever has the boy been doing?" Percival asked his wife.

"Went up the chimney, by the look of it," replied Florence.

"Why?"

"I've no idea, Percival. Boys will be boys."

The Colonel looked smug. "Chip off the old block," he said rather proudly. "I was always an adventurous lad."

But Coco was not the only adventurous one. A few days later it was Hazel who went missing. Coco had gone up. She went down.

Below the ground floor of Ponsonby Place was the cellar, though the door to it was nowadays seldom opened. The flight of steps that led down to the racks where Colonel Sir Percival Ponsonby had kept his wine (when he was a man) was very steep, and the Catlady hadn't been down there for years.

But recently, Mary had taken to using the racks for storing things, and on this particular day she had gone down to fetch some cloths and some shoe polish. Unbeknownst to her, someone else slipped down too.

49

Mary came back up the steep steps and shut the cellar door. She got out Miss Ponsonby's bicycle and set off to do the shopping.

When she returned, she found, once again, the Catlady standing at the front door, leaning on her walking stick. This time, however, she looked delighted, her old face wreathed in smiles.

"Oh, Mary!" she cried. "It's my sister!"

"Your sister?"

"Yes, Hazel. I lost her. I couldn't find her anywhere. But someone else did find her!"

"Who?"

The Catlady pointed down at Vicky, who was sitting at her feet, looking extremely smug.

"Her Most Gracious Majesty found her," said the Catlady. "How Hazel got there I do not know, but she was in the cellar. Somehow she'd been shut in there."

"Oh," said Mary.

"I was getting so worried," the Catlady said. "I looked everywhere, I listened everywhere, but as I think you know, these days neither my sight nor my hearing is what it used to be. I asked Papa and Mama but they didn't seem to understand. And then something extraordinary happened, Mary. Vicky came up to me and put a paw on my stocking—something she has never done

before—and then turned and walked away, stopping and looking back every so often. Clearly, she wanted me to follow her, so I did. She led me to the cellar door, and when I opened it, there was my poor sister sitting on the steps. How glad I was to see her, and so were Papa and Mama and Coco. And how grateful I am to Her Majesty!"

The Catlady bent down and, very respectfully, stroked Vicky's fat ginger back.

"Thank you, ma'am, thank you so much," she said, and Vicky purred loudly.

Percival and Florence, of course, discussed this latest event in their own language.

"How in the world did the girl come to be shut in the cellar?" the Colonel asked his wife.

At that moment, Vicky came into the master bedroom. She was the only cat in the house to be allowed in that room, though normally she spent her days and nights on the Catlady's bed.

Percival and Florence, who had both

been lying on the carpet, sprang up, and Percival stood rigidly to attention like the soldier he had once been.

He waited for Vicky to speak (it was customary among all the cats not to address the Queen first but to wait to be spoken to).

"Well, Colonel," Vicky said, "I trust that your daughter is none the worse for this latest incident?"

"She came to no harm, Your Majesty," Percival replied, "but she might have been imprisoned for a long time had it not been for your skill in finding her, ma'am. My wife and I are truly grateful."

"It was nothing," Vicky said. "We happened to be passing the cellar door and we heard the child mewing. 'Kittens should be seen and not heard,' as the saying goes, but on this occasion it was fortunate that the child cried out."

"And that Your Majesty's hearing is so sharp," said Florence.

"All our five senses are in perfect working order," said Vicky imperiously, and she waddled regally out of the room.

Chapter Six

Probably on account of the Catlady's strangely respectful treatment of Vicky, Mary Nutt began, despite herself, to think quite a lot about this strange idea of reincarnation.

In the Catlady's library she first consulted an encyclopedia. "This belief," she read, "is fundamental to the Hindu and Buddhist concepts of the world."

So millions of people believe in it, she thought. They can't all be barmy. Perhaps Miss Muriel isn't either.

Reincarnation, she read, accounted for the differences in the character of individuals because of what each had once been. So was the fact that Vicky was short and tubby and bossy and that the other cats always let her eat first and seemed to be very respectful toward her—was that all because this ginger cat had once been Queen of England? Rubbish, one part of her said.

Millions believe in it, said another. Of course it would be a comfort to me to be able to believe that my mother and father are alive again, in some shape or form. If only I could, she thought.

I wonder what form Miss Muriel believes she will assume when she dies? Which may not be all that long, she thought. She's aged a great deal in the years that I've been here.

For some time now the Catlady had not come down for breakfast. She ate very little anyway, and Mary, seeing how frail she was becoming, persuaded her to have a tray with a cup of tea and some toast and marmalade brought up to her bedroom.

One morning Mary knocked as usual and took in the tray.

"Shall I pour for you both, Miss Muriel?" she asked.

"Please, Mary dear."

So she saw to the Catlady's tea and then, as usual, filled a saucer with milk and put it on the floor for Vicky.

"How are we today, Miss Muriel?" she asked.

"A little tired. I'm not getting any younger, I fear."

"You stay in bed," Mary said. "I can bring you some lunch up later."

You're really looking very old now, she thought. But not unhappy. Maybe because of this belief of yours that when you die, you'll start again as someone or something else.

"I've been thinking quite a lot," she said, "about what you said to me some time ago. About being reborn, in another body."

"I shall be," said the Catlady firmly.

It still seems odd that she's so sure, Mary thought.

The Catlady did not get up at all that day, saying that she did not have the energy. It was the same all that week, a week that by chance contained two bereavements for Muriel Ponsonby. The cat that had once been her uncle Walter died, and then her old school friend Margaret Maitland.

"Both cats were very old, though, weren't they?" Mary said in an effort to console her friend.

"As I am," said the Catlady.

"Anyway," said Mary, "it's nice for you to think they will both be reborn, isn't it?"

"As I shall be," said the Catlady.

What am I saying? Mary asked herself. I'm barmy too.

She could not make up her mind whether the Catlady was just tired or whether she was ill. And if so, how ill? Should I call the doctor? she thought.

What decided her was a request that the Catlady made.

"Mary dear," she said. "Would you fetch Percival and Florence and Coco and Hazel? I should like to say goodbye to them."

When Mary had done so, she telephoned the doctor. He came and examined the old lady, and then he took Mary aside and said to her, "I'm afraid Miss Ponsonby is very ill. To be honest with you, my dear, I don't hold out much hope."

"She's dying, you mean?" Mary asked.

"I fear so."

Shall I tell him about Miss Muriel's beliefs? she thought. No, he'll think I'm mad as well as her.

The next morning Mary Nutt woke early and dressed. As she went downstairs from her bedroom in what had been the servants' quarters and made her way to the kitchen, she noticed something odd. There was not a cat to be seen, anywhere.

She was about to put a kettle on to make tea when one cat walked in through the kitchen door.

It was Vicky, who stared up at Mary with her customary grumpy look and made a noise that meant, Mary had no doubt, "Follow me."

Up the stairs went Vicky, Mary at her heels, and in through the open door of the Catlady's bedroom.

On the floor, in a rough circle around the bed, were sitting all the other cats of Ponsonby Place: Percival and Florence and their children, Rupert and Madeleine, the newly widowed Aunt Beatrice, Ethel and Edith, and a number of others.

All sat quite still, gazing up at the bed, on which the Catlady lay stretched and still. On her face was a gentle smile.

Mary picked up a hand. It was icy cold. "Oh, Miss Muriel," she whispered. "Who or what are you now?"

Chapter Seven

The vicar was afraid that the funeral of the late Miss Muriel Ponsonby might be very poorly attended. Her mother and father were long dead, he knew (though he did not know that they, and other relatives, still lived, in different shape, in Ponsonby Place). The only mourner he expected to see was Mary Nutt.

What a pity, he thought, that the daughter of Colonel Sir Percival Ponsonby and Lady Ponsonby, of Ponsonby Place, one of the finest old houses in Dummerset, should go to her grave almost unmourned.

In fact, on the day when the Catlady was

buried, the vicar's church was jam-packed.

All the villagers of Dumpton Muddi-corum and all the tradesmen and a number of other people in the neighborhood who owned cats that had once belonged to Muriel, all of these turned up to pay their respects. All the Catlady's oddities were forgotten and only her kindness and cheerfulness remembered.

"She was a funny one," they said, "but there was something ever so nice about her. Always so polite too."

"Yes, and she was a kind lady, taking in Mary Nutt like she did."

Nor were humans the only mourners. At the back of the church, behind the rearmost pews, sat a silent line of cats.

When it was all over, Mary had her tea in the kitchen while on the floor the various cats had theirs (Vicky first, of course). What's to become of me? she thought. I can't stay here now that Miss Muriel's dead. The house will be sold, I suppose.

"I don't know," she said to the cats. "I just don't know."

But a week later, she did.

She was summoned to the offices of the Catlady's solicitor in a nearby town, to be told some astonishing news.

"This, Miss Nutt," said the solicitor, "is a copy of the will of Miss Muriel Ponsonby. As you know, she had no remaining family, no one for whose benefit Ponsonby Place might be sold. She therefore decided that she would leave the house to the RSPC."

"RSPC?" asked Mary.

"The Royal Society for the Protection of Cats. So that the charity might use Ponsonby

Place as its national headquarters. More, the will states that because of your loyal service to her and her deep affection for you, you should continue to live there, rent-free, for as long as you wish. I am delighted to tell you that Miss Ponsonby has left you a substantial sum of money, to cover your day-to-day expenses and to enable you to employ such help as a housekeeper and a gardener. You are a very fortunate young lady."

Fortunate indeed, thought Mary afterward. But oh, how I shall miss her! And so will the cats.

Six months later the RSPC had not yet moved into Ponsonby Place, but Mary, with help, was keeping things in apple-pie order. The only change she made was to remove Vicky from the Catlady's bedroom and Percival and Florence from the master bedroom, and to shut both bedroom doors.

"You'll just have to find other rooms to sleep in," she said to them all, and fat ginger Vicky gave her a look that said plainly, "We are not amused."

Six months to the day from the death of the
Catlady, Mary saw a strange cat come
walking up the drive toward the house, in a
very confident way, as though it knew just
what it was about.

It was a gray cat, about six months old, Mary guessed, with a sharp face and green eyes and rather pointed ears. A female, she was sure, by the look of it.

It walked straight up to her and began to rub itself against her legs, purring very loudly indeed. Then it walked straight in through the front door. Mary followed.

The stranger set off up the stairs and along the landing, to the now closed door of the bedroom of the late Muriel Ponsonby. Standing on its hind legs, it reached up with a forepaw as though trying to turn the door handle.

Mystified, Mary opened the door for it, and it ran into the room and leaped upon the bed. It lay there, ears pricked, its green eyes staring into hers with a look that told Mary Nutt exactly what had happened, something that, up to this moment, she had never quite been able to believe possible.

This strange, green-eyed gray cat, this lady cat, was ... the Catlady!

"Oh, Miss Muriel!" Mary breathed. "You're back!"

THE END

ABOUT THE AUTHOR

DICK KING-SMITH was born and raised in Gloucestershire, England. He served in the Grenadier Guards during World War II, then returned home to Gloucestershire to realize his lifelong ambition of farming. After twenty years as a farmer, he turned to teaching and then to writing the children's books that have earned him many fans on both sides of the Atlantic. Inspiration for his writing comes from his farm and his animals.

Among his well-loved novels are *Babe: The Gallant Pig, Harry's Mad, Martin's Mice* (each an American Library Association Notable Book), *Ace: The Very Important Pig* (a *School Library Journal* Best Book of the Year), *Three Terrible Trins, The Stray, A Mouse Called Wolf, Titus Rules!, The Golden Goose,* and his memoir, *Chewing the Cud*. Additional honors and awards he has received include a *Boston Globe–Horn Book* Award (for *Babe: The Gallant Pig*) and the California Young Reader Medal (for *Harry's Mad*). In 1992 he was named Children's Author of the Year at the British Book Awards. In 1995 *Babe: The Gallant Pig* became a critically acclaimed major motion picture.